Autumn Leaves and Dustbunnys

Kathy G. Carey

AuthorHouse™
1663 Liberty Drive
Bloomington, IN 47403
www.authorhouse.com
Phone: 833-262-8899

ISBN: 978-1-6655-2339-4 (sc)
ISBN: 978-1-6655-2341-7 (hc)
ISBN: 978-1-6655-2340-0 (e)

Library of Congress Control Number: 2021908193

Print information available on the last page.

Published by AuthorHouse 07/15/2021

authorHOUSE

DEDICATION

To my three wonderful Grandchildren,
Phoenix, Kyden and Keelie.

Who gives me inspiration
to keep writing.

AUTUMN LEAVES and DUSTBUNNYS

It's Autumn time, the leaves on the trees changed to such pretty colors. Then the leaves begin to fall to the ground.

The Dustbunny kids are having a fun time. "Watch, out! I am going to jump into the pile of leaves." Nicholas said. Jennifer was throwing leaves up in the air. "Woof, woof!" Dustypup was trying to catch the leaves with his mouth.

Then the kids heard a man name Mr. Gobblestone calling for his cat.

"Hello, Mr. Goblestone, we heard you calling for Autumn is she lost?" Jennifer asked.

"Oh, yes, she is, I'm sure she is so scared. I was racking the leaves in the yard and she was rolling around in them, next thing I knew she was gone." Mr. Gobblestone said. "We will help you look for her." Jennifer said. "Woof!" Dustypup said he was going to help too. "Let's go search for Autumn! Dustypup lead the way." Nicholas said.

It seemed like they have been searching for Autumn the cat for hours. Everyone was getting tired. "Where, could she be?" Mr. Gobblestone said. Jennifer pat him on the back. There is only one thing we can do. "Jennifer and Nicholas bowed their heads and said a prayer. "Dear Lord, we ask that you help us find Mr. Gobblestone's cat Autumn. Please do not let her be afraid. Amen."

Mr. Gobblestone and the Dustbunny kids walked upon a hilltop. There were so many slippery leaves that Nicholas and Jennifer started to slide down the hill. "I'm rolling faster, and faster!" Nicholas said. "Me too!" Jennifer said. Then there went Mr. Gobblestone he was rolling down the hill too. "I'm right behind you kids!"

Rolling down the hill was scary at first, then they started laughing. They landed at the bottom of the hill in a big pile of leaves. "That was fun!" Jennifer said. "I want to do that again." Nicholas said. "I believe, I lost one of my shoes." Mr. Goblestone said. "I think, I found your shoe, I'm sitting on it." Nicholas said.

Then they heard a cat meowing. "That sounds like Autumn." Mr. Gobblestone said. It sounds like it's coming from the tree house." They found Autumn stuck up in the tree house. "Meow!" She was happy to be found. "Autumn! You're alright, I thought we would never find you." Mr. Gobblestone said.

As they were walking home. Mr. Gobblestone said, "I'm so happy we found Autumn or I would be spending Thanksgiving all by myself. Oh, my! The turkey! must be burnt. I was busy looking for Autumn I forgot all about it." They all ran towards Mr. Gobblestone's house. There was black smoke coming from out of the stove. "It's alright, you and Autumn can come to our house for Thanksgiving." Jennifer said.

Mr. Gobblestone and the Dustbunny family were all sitting around the table. Jennifer and Nicholas were telling their mother and father about how Autumn was lost and how they found her. Dustypup and Autumn were eating a piece of pumpkin pie. "Meow, meow!" That means Yummy, yummy in cat language. "Woof, woof!" Means, more please."

The End

Lightning Source UK Ltd.
Milton Keynes UK
UKHW051923230721
387658UK00006B/97